For my sister, Kirsten.

Copyright © 2022 Fiona Halliday

First published in 2022 by Page Street Kids
an imprint of
Page Street Publishing Co.
27 Congress Street, Suite 105
Salem, MA 01970
www.pagestreetpublishing.com

Distributed by Macmillan, sales in Canada by The Canadian Manda Group

21 22 23 24 25 CCO 5 4 3 2 1
ISBN-13: 978-1-64567-348-4
ISBN-10: 1-64567-348-0

CIP data for this book is available from the Library of Congress.

This book was typeset in Athelas. The illustrations were done digitally.
Cover and book design by Melia Parsloe for Page Street Kids

Printed and bound in Shenzhen, Guangdong, China

Page Street Publishing uses only materials from suppliers who are committed to responsible and sustainable forest management.

Page Street Publishing protects our planet by donating to nonprofits like The Trustees, which focuses on local land conservation.

THE LEGEND OF THE STORM GOOSE

Fiona Halliday

PAGE
STREET
KiDS

Erin loved the stories Papa told of his adventures at sea. As they stitched an old white sail to make a kite, he told her the one she loved best.

"The Storm Goose is a great white bird who watches over me when I'm at sea. His wings unfurl to shelter me from storms. He wears a crown of stars so bright I can follow him through the darkest nights. He never rests nor comes ashore."

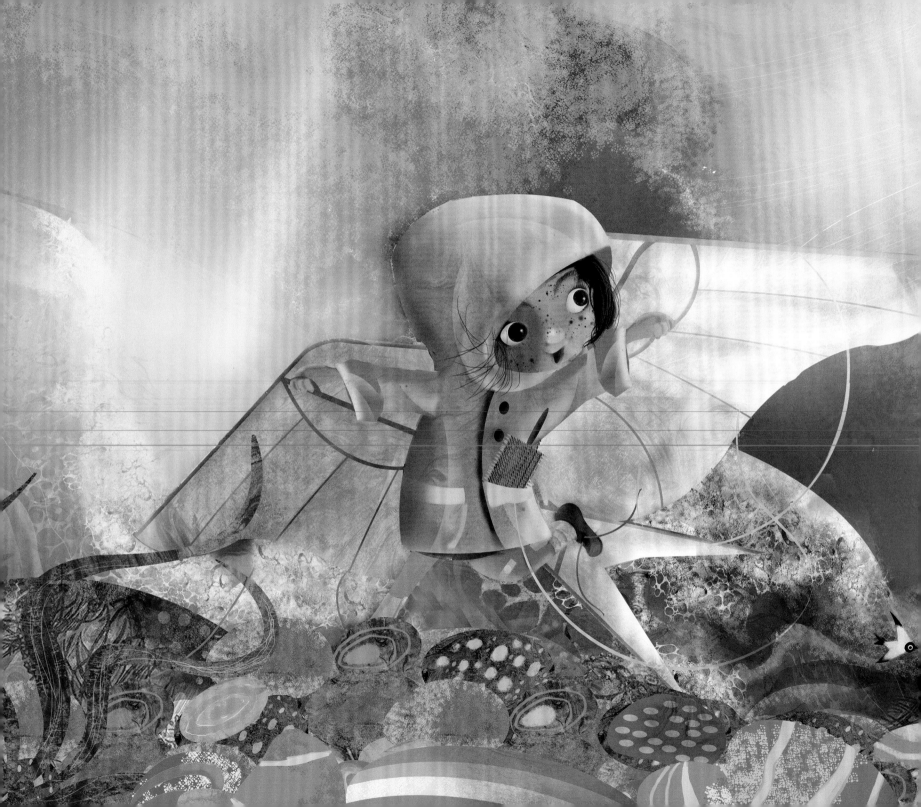

For days after Papa returned to sea, Erin swooped along
the shore. *"Look at the Storm Goose soar!"*

The next Tuesday, black clouds bubbled on the horizon. Waves boiled shoreward. Nana worried, but Erin knew the Storm Goose would keep Papa safe. Erin pressed her nose against the window.

"He watches over Papa. His wings unfurl to shelter him. . . ."

The sea carried a white shape.

"PAPA!"

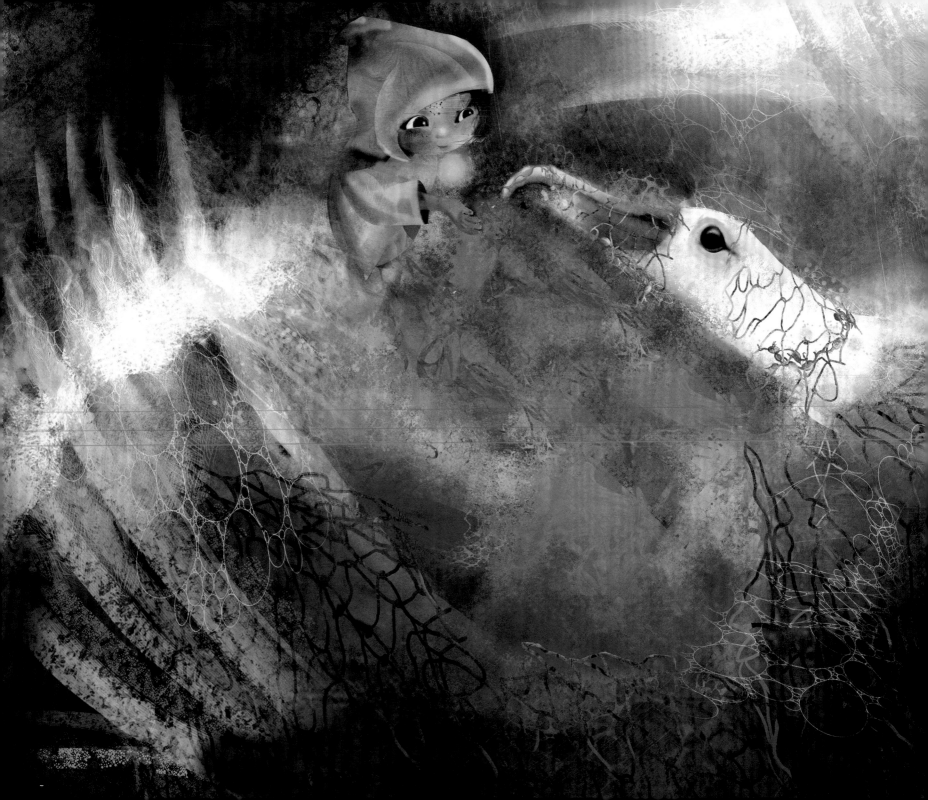

But it was not Papa. Was it the Storm Goose? Where was his crown? And why hadn't he brought Papa? Then she saw the bird was tangled in a net.

"Nana!" she cried, her heart pounding as she tried to free him.

The seaweed squelched under Erin's and Nana's boots as they carried the bird inside. They tended and bandaged him and wrapped him in Papa's favorite blanket.

Clouds of worry gathered in Erin's eyes. Was this exhausted creature really Papa's magical protector? It couldn't be.

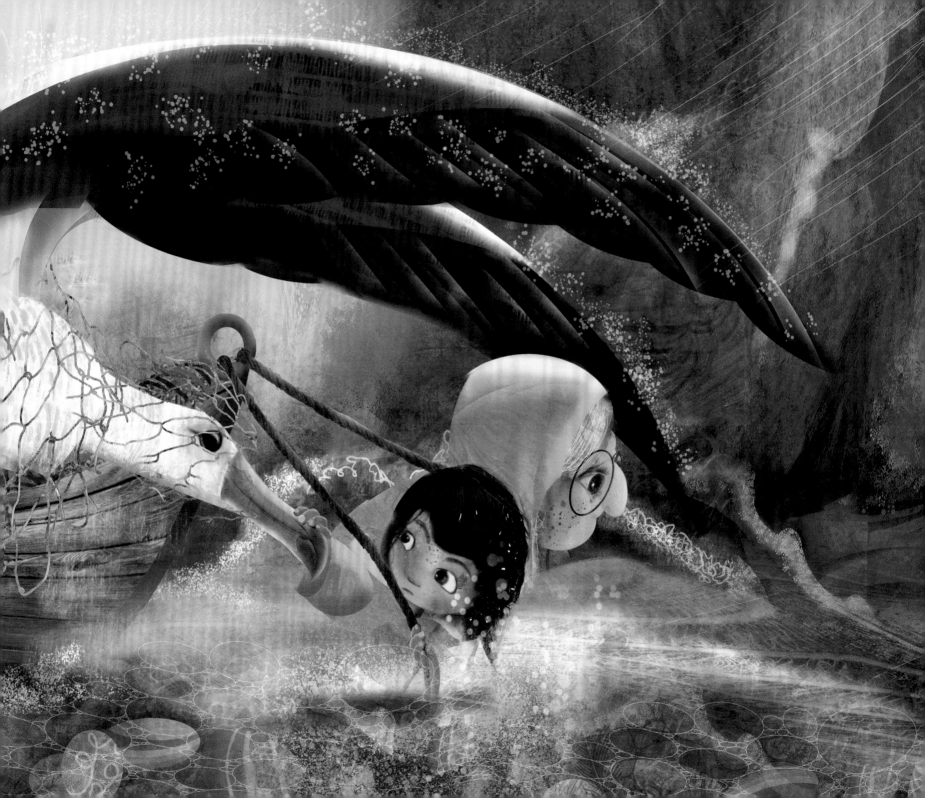

Day after day, Erin perched on the shore, watching for Papa's return. "Come, Erin," Nana said softly, "the Storm Goose needs you!"

But Erin stayed as still as a barnacle on a rock. "There is no Storm Goose." Otherwise Papa would be home by now.

Night after night, she kept her vigil. On the night of the full moon, a soft cry from the sea summoned her over the rocks.

The strange bird had waddled back to the waves. With his broad, flat feet, he paddled a swirling storm of light. When he raised his head, he wore a crown. Just like Papa said!

The bird paddled toward her and dropped glowing stars in her hair. Suddenly, Erin's heart lifted. "You are the Storm Goose! If I can make you better, can we save Papa?"

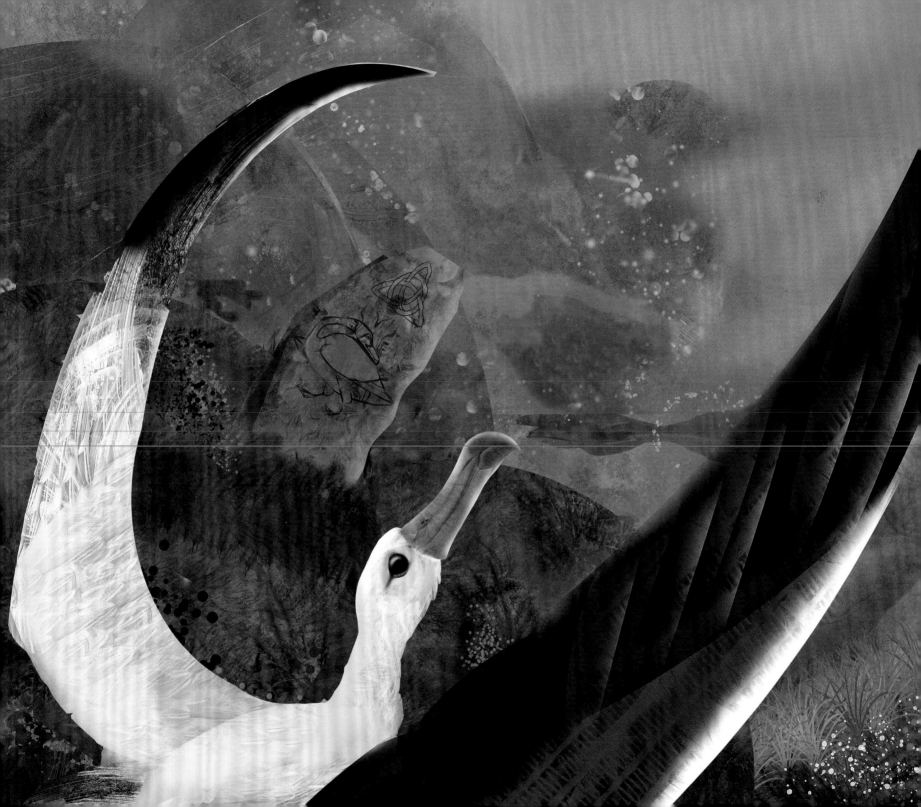

The next morning, ablaze with energy, Erin cut another piece from Papa's old white sail. Two birds danced around Nana. They enfolded her in their long, white wings. Two birds danced through burning puddles of sun. Two birds' wings grew strong again.

Autumn dissolved in shoals of silver flakes. Still the Storm Goose stayed by Erin's side.

"Are you afraid to go? I know you belong in the sky. Even . . . if you don't find Papa." She felt strong enough to say it now.

The wind prowled ever more restlessly. Clouds sailed like pirate flags. The darkness came down again. The Storm Goose's wings arched. They unfurled over Erin. They sheltered her.

And finally, Erin understood. "You came ashore just for me. You came to help me! To tell me . . . Papa is gone."

Then, a flicker of light charged the night. It grew to rippling waves of green. The Storm Goose turned his face to the sky.

"Kurrr!" he cried.

Erin knew the sky was calling him home. But still he hesitated. . . . And if he was here, who watched over the fishermen at sea?

"They need your help more than me now. You can go! Look, follow me!" Erin took a ragged breath. She raced along the shore. She splashed through glittering waves.

She flung her arms wide as if they were her own wings. The Storm Goose followed.

"Goodbye!" she cried.

Then the Storm Goose was gone, and only the clouds remained.

Whenever those clouds became too dark, Erin and Nana huddled together under Papa's favorite blanket, and Erin told the story she loved best:

"*There is a Storm Goose* who watches over me, and though he never comes ashore, he came ashore for me. And though he is strong, sometimes he is weak. And though he needs no help, I helped him. In return, he gave me his wings to lift me out of the dark. There is a Storm Goose. He wears a crown so bright we can follow him through the darkest night."